E
L
O
A
P
Z
M
F
G
I
K
J
C
D
V
X
H
B
T
Y
S
W

Alphabet Wings

Ilana M. Kresner

Lothian
BOOKS

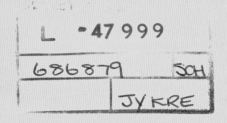

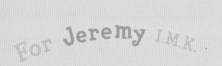

For Jeremy I.M.K.

Thomas C. Lothian Pty Ltd
132 Albert Road, South Melbourne, Victoria 3205
www.lothian.com.au

Text copyright © Ilana M. Kresner 2005
Illustrations copyright © Ilana M. Kresner 2005

First published 2005

National Library of Australia
Cataloguing-in-Publication data:

Kresner, Ilana M.
 Alphabet wings.

 For children.
 ISBN 0 7344 0760 2.

 1. Cities and towns - Juvenile literature. 2. Culture -
 Juvenile literature. I. Title.

307.76

Designed by Georgie Wilson
Colour reproduction by Digital Imaging Group, Port Melbourne
Printed in China by SNP Leefung

I travel the world on my magical alphabet wings.

Allow yourself to be led

To hear, see, taste, touch and smell

In cities from **A** to **Z**.

Here are your alphabet wings.

Let's fly.

Let's zip by **A**msterdam's canals on our bicycles. **Whiz...Whoosh...** what a wonderful way to see the Netherlands.

Come on. We'll ride an elephant to
see Bangkok's floating markets.
Mmm... the smell of sweet
fried banana makes me hungry.
Shall we get some tasty Thai food?
Yum!

Now that we are at the top of the Cairo Tower,
can you see the ancient Egyptian Pyramids of Giza?
Imagine, once the powerful Pharaohs ruled the River Nile.

At the **D**jenné
mosque in Mali,
the African villagers
throw banco to fix
breaks in the walls.

Splat...

a gritty mixture of
mud and rice husk
just landed on my
face.

Listen to the bagpipes at **E**dinburgh Castle in Scotland. The guard is preparing for a performance called the Military Tattoo.

Here is the Ponte Vecchio. It is the most charming bridge in Florence.
Nestled into its sides are shops with sparkling Italian jewellery.

Granada's majestic Alhambra Palace is one of Spain's treasures. Look how the tiles make countless patterns throughout the rooms and courtyards.

Ahh...just in time to watch Hanoi's water puppet performance.

Splash, Rrr, Grr...

The Vietnamese dragon sounds ferocious

as he races across the water.

Have you ever run your fingers over this carpet?
It was made in Turkey; these are
a kind that take years to weave.
I would love to buy one from a
market in Istanbul. Wouldn't you?

Touch the stones of the
Western Wall in Israel's
ancient Jerusalem.
Can you hear the
soft hums
of people praying?

Walk through the ruins
of King Minos' ancient
Palace in Knossos.
Greek legend tells
how the Minotaur,
a half man and half bull,
roared from a labyrinth
under the Palace.

Hurry up!

Hop on that shiny, red
double-decker bus pushing
through London traffic.
We do not want to miss the
changing of the guard at
Buckingham Palace in England.

Count the different colours and shapes on the
outside of St Basil's Cathedral in Moscow.
This is one of Russia's most enchanting buildings.

New York is the busiest city
in the United States of America.
The taxis honk and the lights flash.
Buzz, buzz, buzz.
Beep, beep, beep.
Wow!

We have arrived at The Viking Ship Museum in Oslo, Norway.
snap, snap... make sure you take some good photos of
the magnificent Oseberg and Gokstad ships.

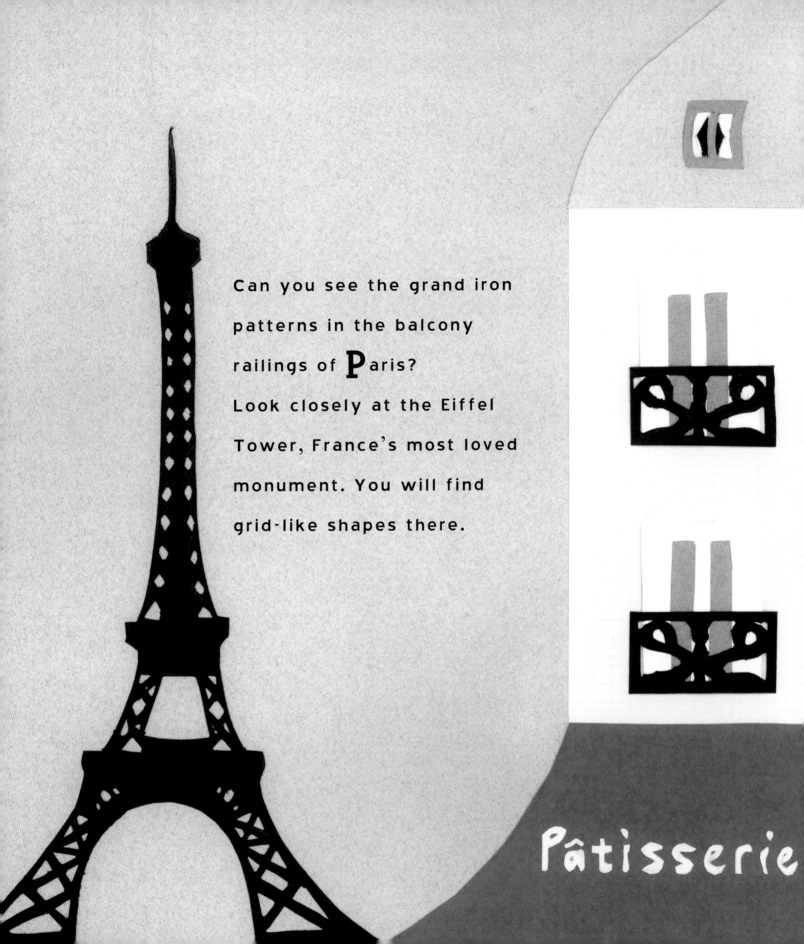

Can you see the grand iron patterns in the balcony railings of Paris? Look closely at the Eiffel Tower, France's most loved monument. You will find grid-like shapes there.

Pâtisserie

Put on your walking shoes so
we can stroll through Quebec's
crowded cobblestone lanes.
Listen to the people speaking
French in this quaint Canadian city.
Bonjour!

Bong, bong. Beat, beat.

Feel the thrilling rhythm of
the colourful Samba dance
in Rio de Janeiro.
It is Carnival time at Brazil's
famous summer festival.

The Sydney Opera House has sails just like the boats on Australia's stunning blue harbour. How relaxing.

Today is the 3rd of March in Tokyo. It is the Japanese Festival of the Girl. Thank you, Kiyoko, for showing us your dolls. We can also fly fish kites during the May Festival of the Boy.

Ushuaia is the most southern city in the world.
Put on your warm clothes before our cruise ship leaves
from this Argentinean port for Antarctica.

Varanasi is a holy city in India. Can you smell the incense? It is where people bathe on the steps in the sacred River Ganges.

Let's watch a rugby match in **W**ellington.
The New Zealanders perform the Maori
Haka dance before the whistle blows.

Ka mate, Ka mate!
Ka ora, Ka ora!

There are over six thousand life-size clay warriors in the X i'an tomb of China's first Emperor. This army will amaze you. Imagine making each warrior.

Indonesia's magnificent Temple of Borobudur is near
Yogyakarta. Locals say that good luck follows those who
touch Buddha's hand or foot.

Zurich is our final stop.
Gobble some of Switzerland's
mouth-watering chocolates as a last treat.

Now we have the energy
to fly home.

We made it from **A** to **Z**.
Please put away your alphabet wings
until the next time we travel together.

See you then.